PUPSTER

Tavio M. Soto

Inspired By: Ariadne Sarai Soto

Devin,
keep being
awesome ?
Nov '22

Editorial Credits:

Sugeil Soto

Melissa Ann Stetson

Cover Art:

Etania Karina

Contact:

For information about this book or to reach the author, email - thepupsterbook@gmail.com.

ISBN-13: 978-1984208224
ISBN-10: 1984208225

Attention Deficit Disorder (ADD)

This story is dedicated to all families that have dealt with the very real symptoms of ADHD/ADD. This book was birthed out of our families struggle to understand our daughter's needs. Ari is her name and she is a remarkable person. She is the inspiration and co-creator of the characters in this book. Sarah encompasses my daughter's sweet and loving spirit.

To all that suffer from this very real disorder…don't stop! Keep working towards your goals. You will accomplish everything that you set your mind to achieve!

--- CONTENTS ---

Chapter 1.	Home Sweet Home	Pg. 1
Chapter 2.	Hunger Pains	Pg. 7
Chapter 3.	Brown Haired Hero	Pg. 13
Chapter 4.	Rude Awakening	Pg. 19
Chapter 5.	A Life Changing Bone	Pg. 23
Chapter 6.	Meeting Killer	Pg. 27
Chapter 7.	Plan B	Pg. 31
Chapter 8.	Live With Monica Snyder	Pg. 37
Chapter 9.	Texas Storm	Pg. 41
Chapter 10.	After the Storm	Pg. 45
Chapter 11.	Waking Up In Heaven	Pg. 51
Chapter 12.	The Fight For Pupster	Pg. 59
Chapter 13.	Dog Napped	Pg. 65
Chapter 14.	Double Caught	Pg. 69
Chapter 15.	The Long Road Home	Pg. 75
Chapter 16.	Sarah's Search	Pg. 82
Chapter 17.	An Unfortunate Rescue	Pg. 86
Chapter 18.	Breaking News	Pg. 90
Chapter 19.	The Deal is Done	Pg. 96
Chapter 20.	Bought & Paid For	Pg. 100
Chapter 21.	The Stroll Home	Pg. 110
Epilogue	Ari's Struggle	Pg. 122

Home Sweet Home

Trust City is a wonderful little town set in the rolling hills of central Texas. On any typical day there is a lot happening. Nearly every shop, from the ice cream parlor to the home-improvement store, is abuzz with shoppers. You can see moms with their children looking at flowers or window shopping at the toy store. On the sidewalks, people are carrying on conversations with old friends. A few dads can be seen drooling over the latest sports cars at the dealership or even discussing the latest baseball stats with a friend at the pizza joint. Teenagers still rode their bikes through the streets to travel to the park to the movie theatre to hangout. Trust City, with it's tranquil setting, seemed like the perfect place to live.

There was one unassuming character that roamed the streets of this serene town. He was a scraggly haired, short legged, happy-tongue hanging out of his mouth, kind of a dog. Nobody really paid him much notice. He would weave in and out of the crowd on his daily walks just as free as the rest of the people. This dog had yet to be named. The last person with whom he had contact with called him *shew*, as in get away from me. That didn't stick though, because it just wasn't a good name for a dog. Honestly, if he had to pick a name for himself, he would have liked to have been called, *The Brave One*, or *Strong and Mighty*. Really, he would've been happy with Spot. But, he had yet to discover his name.

If you haven't figured it out yet, this is the story of a small in stature, yet sprightly dog. What he loves most about his life is that he is completely free. He has no boundaries and no rules. He eats when he wants to eat, he walks where he wants to walk, and pees where he wants to pee.

In fact, he would often stop at the fire department to relieve himself on the fire truck tires. Of course, the fire fighters would catch him. They would get upset and would either yell at him to scat or sometimes...he would get a free shower from the fire hose. This didn't bother him. It was a small price to pay for his freedom. As far as he could tell, life was pretty good.

Life was good but not great. He didn't have a house. He didn't have a family. Up to this point in his life, he didn't even know that having a family was an option for him. Don't feel sorry for him though. As far as he was concerned, he was king of the entire town. He loved it. Everything he needed was at his paws (within reach). For instance, when he would get bored he would chase cats in the back alleys. If he wanted to play with other dogs, he would just head over to the dog walking park. Hunger? No problem! When he was hungry, he would visit the flower shop where the owner would leave him snacks and a bowl of water.

A few buildings down from the flower shop was a Mexican restaurant. It too was an entertaining place.

It could be kind of hostile at times because the owners didn't like seeing him around their establishment. The owner's kids, Juan and Susana, loved having the little dog around to play with. They adored him. They would sneak him leftover soup bones from the kitchen. The kids sometimes got in trouble for feeding him. When they got caught, their mom would chase them around the restaurant with rolled-up newspapers. The kids would run around the tables and laugh while being chased. It wasn't serious trouble. It was a big game that even their mom grew to appreciate.

Another one of his hangouts was the auto repair shop. The owner's name was Big Tex. He was an older man, with a long mustache and a bulging belly. He was known for being grumpy and a man of little words. He snapped at the little dog from time to time, sometimes calling him a *Mangy Mutt*. On the other hand, on cold nights he'd let him sit on his lap, while he pet his head and scratched his back. The nicest thing about the shop was that he had a proper bed in the corner next to a stack of tires. This is where he would go when it rained.

The good thing is that it rarely rained in Trust City, but when it did, it poured. At the edge of town was an empty grass lot. This is where he spent most of his time. It was a very special place. The grass, in this spot, was just high enough to hide him from onlookers and just short enough to allow him to enjoy the cool evening breeze. When he wasn't chasing cats or ducking the rain, he would lay there watching the cars and crowds pass by. Eventually, the streets would go empty and most of the people would disappear. All that remained was his picturesque town and a wide open sky with lots of bright shiny things twinkling back at him. It was the perfect life.

Hunger Pains

The pup woke up early one morning with his belly rumbling. After a routine yawn, stretch, and shake of the leg, he decided to stroll through the neighborhood in search of a bite to eat. He looked and looked but couldn't find any shops open. He walked for hours searching every street, back alley and trash bin without any luck. Not even the Mexican restaurant had any bones placed outside for him. With a deep feeling of sadness, he dropped his head and slowly walked back towards his grass lot. He made it to the edge of town where he decided to rest under a shade tree. Disappointed and hungry he dozed off.

After some time, he woke to the sound of people singing. That is when he realized that he was at the town church. He found himself at the church's annual picnic.

"Ah ha…That's why the town is closed!" he

thought to himself. Then he began his investigation.

The pooch trotted over to a set of double doors to investigate the source of the music. That's when the most amazing smells hit his nose. The aroma of grilled hot dogs, hamburgers, potato salad, grilled chicken and chips filled the air. For a moment, he found himself in a zombie-like state, uncontrollably sniffing out the source of the food.

The wonderful smells were coming from behind a door at the end of the hall. He cautiously made his way to the door being careful not to get caught. He tried pushing open the door with his paw. Then tried to nudge it open with his nose. In a last-ditch effort, he backed his butt up against the door pushing with all his might. His paws slipped and his claws scratched because of the slippery floor. It was impossible for him to get traction. Tuckered out and still hungry he hid under the hallway bench.

He sat for a few moments under concealment

contemplating his next move. What to do? He struggled between two choices. He could stay and continue to try to find a way to the food or he could give up the chase and return to his grassy sanctuary? The sounds of his stomach rumbling were broken by the sound of footsteps approaching from behind the door. He listened intently as the footsteps seemed to be getting closer. When the door swung open, a lady in high heels walked through carrying a plate full of food. His ears stiffened and his eyes welled up with hope as he realized the solution to his problem! He only needed to listen for the next person to come through the door so that he could jump through it when it opened.

He didn't have to wait long. As soon as he heard the next series of footsteps, he prepared his body for a major leap. The light bursting through the door was the trigger. He thrust his body toward the light. He didn't want to miss the opportunity to get closer to the food. The sudden brightness of the light temporarily blinded him, causing him to tumble down a short flight of stairs. He shook off the pain, waiting for his eyes to adjust. That's when he realized that he was outside of the church again. The aroma of the food was all around him. He knew he was close to filling his belly!

He stood up with a new found energy and refocused his attention in the direction of his goal. He spotted the picnic tables. The tables were full of all kinds of goodies. He fixed his gaze on a large plate of plump, juicy, steamy hot dogs. A trance like state overpowered him as the hunger pains took control of his senses. He crouched down like a lion tracking his prey. Nothing was going to stop him now.

He looked left, then right, took in a deep breath…then exhaled. With every ounce of energy remaining in his weakening body, he thrust himself toward the plate of hot, steamy, delicious weenies. Dirt flew from the tips of his paws as he charged toward the goal. His eyes remained stern and focused.

As he approached the food, his concentration melted from instinct to anticipation. His focused look morphed into an optimistic smile. His tongue slipped out of his mouth causing slobbery drool to fly past his ears. With one final kick, he was in the air. This was it! He closed his eyes and opened his mouth big and wide.

"Chomp!" the dog's jaws clamped down with a wrenching sound of chattering teeth.

A man dressed in a black suit held caught him in mid-air. He looked at the pup shaking his head and telling him, "Not today little one." Then he placed him under a large milk crate under the canopy of the oak tree.

Smelling the food from his makeshift jail was extreme torture. He peered out the holes of the crate staring at the food. All he could do was cry.

Brown Haired Hero

So, there he was, hungry, locked up, and crying. All the dog wanted was to fill his empty tummy with a few hotdogs. To make matters worse, the church service ended and the people came out and ate up all the food.

"Let me out!" he cried. "Please, just one hotdog and then I'll go home! Please..." He begged but nobody paid him any attention.

The little pup feared for his life. He was trapped and all alone. In the midst of this confusing and frustrating moment, something happened that he would never forget. The most beautiful site that he had ever seen walked up to him. His fear gave way to curiosity as he watched her take a seat next to him. He stopped crying and looked up at the little girl. She was about the age of ten. She had dark brown hair and a beautiful smile. She wasn't like the group of boys who poked him with sticks. He felt deep in his heart that this girl was special. She began a conversation.

"Are you having a bad day?" she asked.

He was weak from a lack of food and still stunned that someone was being nice to him. He remained still, looking back at her with a curious gaze.

She rambled on. "My name is Sarah. Do you have a name? The other kids aren't nice to me." she continued with a sad tone. "That's why I spend a lot of time alone. My parents are over there talking to the pastor. Are you hungry?"

He responded by looking at her with the biggest, saddest, puppy eyes and gave out a yelp. "Yelp!"

Sarah got up and ran towards the picnic table. It wasn't long before she returned with a plate of food. She placed it on the ground, looked around to ensure nobody was looking, then put a hotdog through the gap. The dog wasn't shy. He snatched up the hotdog so fast that it startled Sarah, forcing her to quickly yank her hand back. Two bites and it was gone.

Sarah laughed. She sat down next to him leaning on the tree. She began pulling apart a cheeseburger, dropping the pieces through the top of the crate. They too, were gobbled up quickly. She continued her one-sided conversation with her new friend. Distracted by her stories she scraped some coleslaw off the plate to share with her new friend.

The dog looked at the slaw, smelled it and barked in disapproval. "Bark!"

Sarah gave out a hearty laugh, "I'm sorry little guy. I didn't like the slaw either." She fed him another hotdog. With his belly full, he moved to the side of the crate closest to his new friend, allowing Sarah to pet his head. It was the most amazing feeling for the both of them.

"I wonder if you have a name? I bet you don't. I'll call you Pupster, on account that you look like a puppy and have a brown spot on your paw that sort of resembles a star."

The serene moment was broken up by the hollering of a concerned parent. "Abigail Sarah Snyder! Get away from that dirty thing! You don't know where it's been!" A man's voice shouted over the crowd.

"That's my dad. I better go. It was nice meeting you. I want you to know that you made today a very special day for me. Bye Pupster. I'll be thinking of you, my friend." She looked back and gave a final wave then ran to return to her parents.

Just as quickly as she came into his life, she was gone. With a newly found strength he was able to think straight. It was time to come up with an escape plan. He looked around surveying his makeshift prison cell. He saw a large rock on the top of the crate. It was much too heavy to move it or to knock it over. His only chance to escape seemed to be to dig.

He began digging in the lowest area that he could find. He made a hole just big enough for his head to fit through. It would be just enough. He pushed, squeezed and pulled himself through. He made it! He was free!

Finally, free of his cage, Pupster ran from the church picnic grounds without looking back. He darted straight for the safety of his grassy home, taking with him two things; a new identity and memories of a new friend. No longer was he an insignificant, dirty little dog. Now, he had a name! His name was Pupster. As he ran from the church, visions of his new friend danced through his mind. He hoped to see her again.

Rude Awakening

Pupster made it back to his grassy haven just before darkness had fallen on the city. He found the tallest weeds to knock down in order to make a bed. Walking in a circle he trampled them down until a makeshift nest was formed. He was completely camouflaged. Now, he was safe. As the sounds of the city began to subside, he drifted away into a deep sleep.

His paws twitched as he entered into a deep sleep. He was dreaming of his new friend Sarah. In this dream, they were walking side-by-side at the city park. She stopped about every ten steps or so to feed him a doggy treat. Around his neck was a golden collar that glistened in the sunlight. Etched into the dangling tag was his name, PUPSTER. They were both very happy, walking, talking, and playing. All was perfect in his dream.

The serene moment began to give way to a dark smokey haze. Suddenly, a swarm of giant mosquitoes started chasing them. The park transformed into a dark forest. They found themselves running, dodging trees, and ducking under limbs. They ran as fast as their legs could carry them in order to escape the BUZZING... WIZZING... ZOOMING, of the swarm. The BUZZING got louder with every second! Their hearts pounded as they tried to get away. The insects circled them sweeping closer and ZOOMING tighter with each pass!

Sarah was panicky, trying to find a way out of the twisted situation. She bent down and swooped up Pupster in her arms. Her gaze scanned back and forth in search of a sanctuary. The mosquitoes were nearly upon them! She jumped over a log only to have her shoelace get caught on a protruding limb. Sarah crashed to the ground. The force of the fall ripped Pupster from her arms. He tumbled into a tree. He immediately found his footing and looked back at

Sarah. She was surrounded! The swarm had swallowed her. She tried to swat the insects away but it was too late. With her final breath she screamed, "PUPSTER GET UP! … RUNNNNNNNNN!!!"

From his deep sleep, he sprang to his feet. Pupster frantically looked in all directions for Sarah. Still groggy, it only took a moment for him to realize that he was dreaming. If he was dreaming, then where was the BUZZING sound coming from? From within the tall grass he heard the loud noise coming straight for him! A riding lawn mower was heading straight for him. He leaped for safety, barely dodging the clenches of the deadly mower blades. Still in shock, he stammered across the street.

After a few moments, his heart beat returned to normal. From the safety of the sidewalk, he watched as his home was destroyed. He nervously watched as the city workers cleared the lot of all vegetation. After the grass was cleared, then the heavy trucks rolled in. Surveyors placed cones, measured distance-points and marked the dirt with orange paint. His sanctuary was gone.

Pupster was now officially homeless. He turned away from the lot and slowly walked down the sidewalk in disbelief. For the first time in his life, he truly felt alone.

The stroll gave him time to reflect on what had just occurred. Images of Sarah kept popping into his mind. Then he recalled his dream. Had she not told him to get up and run, he would have been a goner! He would have died! He was trying to make sense of it all.

Pupster found himself at the Mexican restaurant. He quietly made his way to the alley-side of the shop. He took refuge under a set of stairs. He had a lot to think about. What was he going to do now?

A Life Changing Bone

A pair of voices startled Pupster out of his sleep. "Here puppy puppy. Come here puppy. We have a bone for you."

The kids tried their best to coax Pupster out from underneath the stairs. Pupster was not budging. He was not in the mood. He laid there motionless, staring at them as they tried their best to pull him out to play. After a few minutes they gave up trying. Susana tossed the bone in front of him.

"Bye Puppy, we have to go now. Bye!" The siblings ran off to catch up with their parents who were waiting at the front of the store.

Pupster stared at the bone. It looked enticing, but he was too distracted to eat. Pupster was sad about losing his home. He was also upset that he didn't know when he would see Sarah again, if ever.

After a few minutes, he returned his attention to the bone. He inched forward nudging it with his nose. He thought he might as well have a nibble while trying to figure out what to do with his life. Licks gave way to gnawing. Before long, the bone was half eaten.

The snack was a great distraction. It allowed him to free his mind so that he could figure out what to do with the sudden changes in his life. He had a couple of options. First, he could choose to live under the stairs at the restaurant. This choice certainly presented some perks. His second choice was living at the auto shop with grumpy Big Tex. Living with him would probably be the best option. It would provide a good home until he could make other arrangements. His mind was set. He was off to the auto shop.

Pupster had one more matter of business to take care of before leaving. He needed to find a good hiding place for his bone. He decided to bury it. He took it to the trees in front of the restaurant where he quickly planted his bone. With a final tap on the dirt he secured it's safety.

He was feeling much better. With a new sense of purpose, he strolled down the road to his new residence. He was reinvigorated and ready to take on the world. Nothing could keep him down!

After a few minutes, he arrived at the shop. He peeked through the big open doors. Big Tex was out. The lights were off. The old car that was in pieces in the corner was still where he remembered it. The old beat-up sofa that sat in front of an old tube-style television also hadn't been moved. Everything seemed to be in order.

Pupster cautiously entered the dim room looking around to make sure it was safe. He walked to his corner and found his bed. Next to the bed were bowls with fresh food and water.

"This was new," he thought. "Wow...Tex really does like me!"

As he nibbled on the food, he could not have been happier. After eating, he laid down for the night.

Chapter 6

Meeting Killer

From what seemed far away, Pupster heard an angry, snarling voice, "Hey you! Get out of my bed."

Pupster's eyes remained closed, dismissing the voice as a figment of his imagination.

He heard the voice again, this time much closer and much angrier, "If you don't get up and move out of my bed right now, I am going to hurt you!"

A piercing pain in his neck forced Pupster's eyes open. He found himself in the clutches of an angry German Shepherd. The massive dog flung his head around, trying to do as much damage to Pupster as he could. With each powerful twist, his teeth burrowed deeper into Pupster's skin, ripping his fur, causing him to yelp in pain. In one vicious motion, he flung Pupster across the room.

Pupster bounced off the side of the broke down car. Blood seeped from his wounds. He frantically looked around for help. Before he had a chance to make a move, the Shepherd was on him again.

The Shepherd hovered over Pupster. "How dare you get into my bed while I was away." Drool dribbled off his mouth as he snarled, exposing his teeth. He continued, "I don't know who you are, but you have a lot of guts to come into my home, eat my food, drink my water and sleep in my bed. You are dead meat!"

Pupster tried to explain who he was and why he was there, but the vicious dog was blinded by rage. The aggression continued as the powerful dog gnashed his teeth and chomped at him again. Pupster ducked the bite, and darted underneath the angry dog's belly. The Shepherd kicked him with his hind leg as Pupster tried to escape. Pupster stumbled into the wall. He knew he was outmatched. He closed his eyes anticipating the final blow.

A booming voice from an adjacent room broke up the attack. "What's going on back there? Killer, what'd you catch?" Big Tex came stumbling into the room. "Down boy, let me see what you got." Tex forced his way in between Killer and his prey.

Pupster had never in his life been so happy to hear that grumpy man's voice! Tex knelt down, picked up Pupster, and looked over his injuries. All the while, Killer was snarling and growling.

"GET BACK!" yelled Tex.

Killer moved to the back of the room pacing back and forth, waiting for another chance to attack.

With a remorseful tone, Big Tex spoke to Pupster, "Well...darn. I am so very sorry bud." He grabbed a dirty rag from the counter and wiped some of the blood off of his fur. Pupster winced as his wounds were cleaned. He looked up at Tex and back at Killer. He knew that this relationship was now over.

With Pupster cradled in his arm, Big Tex walked over to the door. He gently placed Pupster on the ground. In his southern accent, he told his injured friend, "Good bye boy. Don't come back. I have a new watch dog. This place isn't safe for you no more." Then he slid the door shut.

Pupster watched through the glass door as Tex walked away. His heart broke as he watched Killer receiving a pat on the head as Big Tex walked past him to sit in his chair.

He whimpered in pain, mustering up just enough strength to stand. He slowly hobbled away leaving behind a small trail of blood. His silhouette faded into the morning fog.

Plan B

Pupster was in bad shape. Emotionally, he was broken. Life had just dealt him two difficult blows. He didn't know what to do next. With nowhere else to go, Pupster decided to find refuge at the park.

As he approached the park, he noticed the weather was starting to clear. The fog had dissipated. Once the sun broke through the clouds, it warmed up the day. He found himself at the pond, where the ducks were carrying on with their usual routine. They were in a tussle with the geese. A small crowd of people had already gathered to feed the water fowl from the bridge. The ducks and geese always fought for the best position to get the biggest scraps.

Pupster quietly strolled into the water for a quick bath and to wash off the blood from his fur. He hesitantly tiptoed into the pond from the shallow bank. Once he was comfortable with the temperature, he paddled out to the deep.

He swam around for a bit. The water was refreshing. The blood washed off while the cool water helped to reduce the swelling of his wounds.

Once he felt better, he dove under the water looking up at the ducks feet. It was an amazing view. The sun shone through the glistening water top. The duck's and geese's feet paddled away, creating ripples in the water. Through the refraction of sunlight, you could also see the people feeding the ducks and geese. A lot was happening. Pupster swam up to the gaggle from under the water. He popped up in the middle of the group. They responded with squawking and pecking. Clearly, this was a very bad idea.

The playful moment was broken by a splash, followed by the screaming of human voices. People shouted and scrambled to get to the pond. It was a moment of shear confusion. Pupster wondered what had fallen into the water.

A woman screamed, "Over there! Quickly! Someone do something! Hurry or else the girl is going to drown!" She pointed towards Pupster's direction.

A man, dressed in a suit, yelled, "Call the police and the fire department!" He too searched frantically from the shore.

The ducks and geese flew away, frightened by the ordeal. Pupster was the closest so he began his search. Not quite sure what he was looking for, he dove beneath the water in search of anything out of the ordinary. That's when he spotted a young girl drifting to the bottom of the pond. He didn't have enough air to reach her. He returned to the surface for a quick breath then went back under. This time he was able to get to her. He clamped on to her jacket sleeve with his teeth. He swam with all his strength towards the surface of the water. He finally made it, cresting the water with the girl in tow.

"There she is!" Someone shouted from the bridge. "That dog pulled her up!"

Pupster realized that her head was still under water. He let go of her sleeve, took a breath and went under again. She started to sink. He caught her, grabbing on to her jacket collar this time, pulling her head above the water.

As soon as the couple saw their daughter, they jumped into the pond. The man and woman plunged into the water, feet first, from bridge. They landed just a few feet from Pupster and the girl. They grabbed her and swam to the shore. One of the rescuers began CPR while the other prayed.

"Come on Sarah!" the dad pleaded. "God, please help. Give me my daughter back." With those words, the little girl spit up some water and gasped for air. "Thank you God!" He said crying as he scooped up his daughter to take her to the hospital.

Pupster swam away from the scene. He reached the shore on the opposite side of the pond. He shook off the water upon exiting the pond, completely unaware of the severity of the situation. He walked off towards the picnic area in search of food. He had no idea that the girl he helped retrieve was the same girl that befriended him at the church picnic.

In a dazed state, Sarah pointed at the dog on the opposite side of the pond. She called out his name, "PUPSTER…" then collapsed from the stress of her ordeal.

Live With Monica Snyder

"This is Monica Snyder reporting on the events that transpired earlier in the day. An amazing, yet surreal tale unraveled this afternoon as my daughter accidently fell from the bridge during the annual 'Duck Day' event. It was a very traumatic experience for our family." Monica, Sarah's mom, did her very best reporting the news while holding back her tears. "Thankfully, Sarah is doing fine. She is recovering at home. The doctor says that she was pulled from the water just…in…time…" She paused for a moment, again holding back her emotions. "Well, in any case, she is good!" Monica was relieved to have made it through the first part of her report.

Her co-anker spoke up to allow her to gain her composure. "The most significant part of this story is how Monica's daughter was rescued. Somewhere out there is a little dog that, literally, came from the depths of the pond to assist in the rescue of Sarah.

Where did the dog come from? Who does he belong to? There are many questions that still need answered in this unraveling mystery. Wouldn't you say Monica?"

Finally, with her emotions mostly in check, Monica responded. "Indeed, that is true George. The news station is taking calls from anyone who has information about our little hero dog."

When she spoke the words, *hero dog*, she broke down in tears. She couldn't help it. The mystery dog saved her baby girl's life.

She closed out her segment in tears. "If anyone has any information on the whereabouts of this dog please call the station. Please call me. I, I mean, we would like to personally thank the owner of this special dog who saved our daughter."

George continued the report. Looking towards Monica, "Thank you Monica. We are all grateful for your daughter's recovery." Returning his attention to the camera, "Please take a look. This is the only known image of the dog." He held up a picture from a reporter who accidently snapped a shot of Pupster in the background of the rescue scene. The picture showed Pupster walking away from the pond, while looking back at the crowd.

The camera panned out to focus on George the co-anker. "This dog was last seen leaving the pond walking towards the picnic area of the park. Finally, the city Mayor has taken notice of this heroic act. He would like to personally bestow a Medal of Heroism upon this miracle dog. If you have any information pertaining to his identity, please, contact us." Without skipping a beat, he changed subjects. "Coming up after the break, the high school drama club presents their adaptation of Grease, and yes, Grease is still the word!"

George's attempt to tell a joke went unnoticed. The only thing that was on anyone's thoughts was trying to find the identity of the mysterious dog who saved Sarah. The hunt was on!

Texas Storm

Although his stomach was empty, Pupster was extremely tired. He was exhausted from pulling the little girl out of the pond, and still in pain from his altercation with Killer. He took refuge under a bunch of shrubs. He fell asleep licking his wounds.

Pupster awoke the next morning to the distant sounds of rumbling in the sky. As he shook off his grogginess, he noticed the sun giving way to dark clouds. It looked like it was going to rain. He strolled through the park trying to find a more suitable spot to take cover from the weather. After a few moments, he discovered a shiny round disk with plenty of space underneath that should keep him dry. He dug a nook beneath the merry-go-round. It was perfect. Now, he was shielded from both the rain and the wind.

Thunder echoed through the sky. It was the beginning of a major thunderstorm. Without warning, it began to pour. The wind kicked up and tossed the trees back and forth. Then lightning flashed. It was followed by resounding thunder that shook the park. The storm rolled in with such force that it frightened Pupster.

The rain gave way to hail. Frozen balls of ice, the size of nickels, pelted the metal merry-go-round. The repeated heavy dings made his head hurt. Pupster's fear was quickly turning to panic! He was cold, tired, injured and hungry. "When would his nightmarish week end?" he thought.

He peered out from beneath the steel saucer. At that very moment, lightning struck the ground next to the playground. His sanctuary was no longer safe. He had to find a safer place to get out of the storm. Pupster decided that the best place to be would be the Mexican restaurant. He had to move quickly.

"Be strong..." he told himself. "One... two... three..." On three, Pupster dashed from under his safe haven, immediately being struck by hail. He winced in pain but kept going. He ran in a zigzag motion in an attempt to avoid the icy stones. He ran as fast as his legs would take him, seeking refuge under whatever cover he could find.

CRASH! A bolt of lightning exploded, striking a tree limb above his head. Pupster jumped out of fright from the sudden jolt of light and the resounding sound of thunder. Sparks flew as the branch broke. It fell directly in Pupster's path. He tried to avoid the danger. It fell right on him, knocking him to the ground. He was pinned between the ground and the weight of the limb. He fought as much as he could, but he wasn't able to free himself. The final blow came when a ball of hail, the size of a golf ball, struck him on the head. He was knocked unconscious. He laid motionless, pinned, and partially buried in mud. The rain poured and hail relentlessly pelted his body.

It looked as if this really was the end for Pupster.

After the Storm

"Come on John." The supervisor of the clean-up crew shouted to his worker. "Pick up those branches and move the debris to the collection site." He pointed at some damage as he continued his statement. "Boy am I glad there wasn't any children on that merry-go-round." He was referring to the mangled mess of metal that used to be the merry-go-round. The lightning had struck the ride, completely destroying it, and also burned the grass all around. "Man this park looks like a war zone."

In every direction, all that was visible was the wake of destruction, trash and fallen trees.

A man, dressed in dirty jeans and an orange vest, stood next to the remains of a fallen tree. He didn't move. He just stood silently, staring at something on the ground. He appeared to be crying. He took off his hard hat, slowly tapping it on his leg.

Monica and her cameraman were on the scene to do a story on the storm. It was the worst storm to hit the town in over a hundred years.

"Monica, look over there! What's that man doing?" asked her cameraman, pointing towards the worker hovering over something.

"I don't know. It looks like we might have a scoop on something. Aim the camera towards him to see if you can capture what he is looking at." responded Monica.

He zoomed in as close as he could. Through the lens of the cameraman, he panned down to the ground to catch a glimpse of what the man was viewing. "Oh, no...it can't be!" he mumbled under his breath. "Is it him?"

"Is it who?" asked Monica. "What is it?"

"We need to head over there and get a better look. This may be the story that you were looking for. I really hope it isn't but...it doesn't look good."

"What is it?" she demanded.

"You'll see!" he replied with a sad tone. They both walked over to where the man was. They stood beside him. As they looked down at the apparent lifeless animal, they all fell silent in a moment of extreme sadness.

Lying lifeless before them was the hero dog that everyone was looking for.

Monica, in a devastated tone, told the cameraman, "Cut the feed. This isn't the story that I want to share." She knelt down beside the lifeless body and cried. Reaching down she caressed his head. "Little dog. Please come back. Our town needs you. My daughter needs you. You can't leave us yet. But, if it really is your time..," she moved in closer to whisper towards Pupster's ears, "I want you to know that I love you. Thank you for saving my daughter." Monica kissed him, then stood up. She wiped her tears and motioned the cameraman to wrap it up. Wit very heavy hearts they walked away from the scene. The commotion attracted a crowd. The mood was somber. Everyone that gathered was extremely troubled.

"I can't believe it!" Exclaimed the worder in a deep voice. "It's okay boy. Don't move. We got you!" One of the clean-up crew members hovered over Pupster while another shouter, "Call an ambulance, I mean a vet. Somebody call somebody that can help!"

In response to the commotion, Monica and the cameraman whipped around to see what was happening. The cameraman threw the camera onto his shoulder and hit record before Monica had a chance to direct him. They ran back pushing through the group of people who gathered to view Pupster. Monica stood beside the worker, who had taken off his vest to cradle the little dog. Pupster was unconscious but breathing.

Monica began her interview. With tears of joy rolling down her cheeks, she made a public plea for anyone watching, to pray for the little hero dog.

After a short conversation with the workers, Monica was able to negotiate for the custody of Pupster. At the end of the day, Monica found herself in the veterinarian's office caring for the helpless, wounded mutt.

The veterinarian addressed Monica. "Monica, it is very nice to finally meet you. I watch your segment every day."

"Thank you. Really, the pleasure is all mine," she replied.

"So, this is one lucky dog. He has some very deep bruises and a massive knot on his head. The good thing is, he didn't break any bones. I would like to keep him sedated for a couple of days to make sure he doesn't hurt himself. Would that be alright?"

"Yes, of course."

"Do you have any idea who the owner may be?"

"No, I don't. If it's alright, I would like to take him home. I'll do a news story to see if we can find the owner."

The doctor was pleased with her response. "Sounds like a plan. Please check in anytime. He'll be ready to be released on Friday. Good luck with the search. I bet there are a lot of people who are going to want take this little lucky charm home!"

Waking up in Heaven

"What's going on? Where am I? Why am I so dizzy? Ouch, ouchee, owee…my head hurts!" Pupster began to wake up from his doctor induced coma. "The last thing that I remember is that I was at the park. It was hailing and I was running. That's the last thing I remember," he thought to himself. He looked around realizing that he was in someone's home. "I'm in a house? Wow! This is a nice house with walls and a roof."

He looked down at the floor at a shiny metal bowl with some letters on it. "What is this? A bowl of food and water? Oh my..." As his senses slowly crept back, he found that the ground beneath him was squishy and soft. "What is this? Was I sleeping on a pillow?"

In light of what happened with Killer, he was a little apprehensive about making any movements toward the food. He looked around but didn't see or hear any other animals. He sniffed around the food. "I sure am hungry. I hope this food is for me. The last time I was in this predicament I almost got eaten."

He very cautiously nibbled at the food, looking around each time he put his head down in the bowl. After a few minutes, he let his guard down and dug in deep. He chomped and slobbered and chewed. He was so hungry that he forgot where he was. He didn't even notice the people watching him from the other room.

Sarah giggled. "Look mom. He is awake. It looks like he is okay. He sure is hungry! Is it okay that he is making a mess? I know you don't like me to eat like that!"

"Hush!" Her mom responded, gently placing her hand on her daughter's lips. "Let him eat. We don't want to disturb him while he is eating. He might bite."

"Oh Mommy, he'll never bite me. I promise. Are we going to keep him?"

"Well Baby, we have to see if he has an owner first. I am going to use my position to create a news story to see if someone claims him. If he doesn't have a home, then maybe we can keep him."

At this news, Sarah became very nervous. The last thing she wanted was to have to give up Pupster to a stranger. Sarah looked up at her mom, her eyes welling up with tears. "But Mom, he saved my life. He should stay here. Don't you think so?"

Monica understood her daughter's pain but knew that she had to try to find the owner. "It's not that simple, baby girl. Let's just see what happens." Monica kissed Sarah on the forehead.

Once Pupster finished his food he went for some water. He remained completely oblivious to his viewers. He drank the water just as quickly as he ate the food. Once satisfied, he began his exploration. He stumbled his way around the kitchen sliding on the hard wood floors and bumping into cabinets. It wasn't long until he found the living room. That's when he noticed the people watching him. He slowly scanned the people from their feet to their faces. That's when it happened. Sarah and he locked eyes for the first time since the church picnic.

Sarah shrieked out of excitement.

Monica waited nervously to see what the dog was going to do.

Pupster was frozen. He didn't think this was possible. He thought for a moment that he was dreaming.

Sarah kneeled down and spoke. "Come here boy." Her voice broke Pupster's trance, freeing him to run to the arms of his best friend. He ran to her, practically jumping into her arms. He licked and kissed her and yelped in excitement.

Monica relaxed, sighing in relief that Pupster

remembered Sarah. She cherished this moment. She took out her phone snapping several pictures of their reunion.

Sarah and Pupster had a great time. She picked him up and showed him all around the house. She showed him her room, her favorite toys, and she even moved his doggy pillow to the foot of her bed.

Pupster was so excited. He didn't know how to process everything. For the first time in a long time, he was sure of two things. He was safe and happy. He also knew that he didn't want to be away from his best friend.

After the passing of several hours the pair noticed something happening in the living room. The news crew was setting up their gear. Sarah directed Pupster to follow her to the living room. "Come on Pupster. My mom is going to do an interview with you."

Monica began the tone with a very serious tone.

She spoke directly to the camera. "I am Monica Snyder reporting live from my living room. I am here with our very own hero dog. As most of you know, this dog pulled my daughter from the pond. He saved her life." Monica's voice cracked. She paused to gain her composure and wiped her tears.

The camera moved off of Monica to focus on Sarah and Pupster. Sarah smiled and waved to the invisible audience. Monica continued talking. "My daughter gave this special friend of hers a name, she calls him Pupster. Along with the name, we were able to give back to him that which he gave to us. We nursed him back to life after discovering that he was struck by a tree in the storm that destroyed the park. He has been here with us recovering ever since. If you are the owner, or know who the owner may be, please come forward. We can be reached at 555-2323 or come by the news station to speak with one of our managers. Thank you for watching this special report. I am Monica Snyder with Chanel 7 News, stay tuned for all your local updates!"

The response from the public was almost immediate. The Snyder's received so many phone calls that they had to have the phone number forwarded to the news station. Several volunteers gathered to take the phone calls. Hundreds of people called in wanting to claim Pupster as their own. They compiled the information and followed up with all credible leads.

So many people wanted him that it was too difficult to determine who, if any of these people, he really belonged to. Of all the claims there was one that seemed quite convincing. Big Tex, the owner of a local car repair shop, claimed that Pupster lived in his shop. He followed up his phone call with a visit to the station, taking a few of his customers with him to corroborate his claim.

The Fight For Pupster

The whole town was abuzz over the news that Pupster had no family. It seemed as if everyone wanted to take him home. People could be heard arguing from the barbershop to the burger joints. There was a long line at the television station of people wanting to prove that they were the 'rightful' owner of Pupster. The police arrived to assist with settling the town dispute. They took control of Pupster until they could figure out what to do.

Sarah watched from the front door as the police officers carried Pupster away in a cage. Pupster was clearly scared. There was no way for him to know why he was being taken away. As soon as the police car drove off, she ran to her dad crying. "Why did they have to take him away?"

He kneeled down and pulled her into a great big hug. "Baby Girl!" he stated quietly. "We talked about this. There is a good chance that Pupster isn't even his name. He could have an owner who calls him by a different name..."

Before he could finish his thought, Sarah interrupted him, sobbing. "It's not true daddy. I know for sure. Remember the church luncheon. He is the little dog that I was feeding. He did not have a collar. He doesn't have a home. I just know it! He belongs with us!"

As Sarah's dad attempted to calm her down, the city officials were trying to figure out how to deal with Pupster. The city council called a special session to discuss the issue. It was decided that there would be a town hall meeting presided over by Judge Carter. Judge Carter would have the final say on the matter. The event was set for Friday, the location would be the court house.

The news spread to neighboring towns. It was shared on social media. Even the national networks were reporting on the spectacle. The once insignificant little dog was now a national super star. Friday came quick. News affiliates from all across America arrived to witness the proceedings.

The atmosphere in the courthouse was dense and serious. The room was packed. Sarah and her parents sat in the front row. Everyone was extremely quiet. It was as if the town had shut down to give its full attention to determining who the hero dog's family would be. All eyes were on Judge Carter.

Judge Carter opened the proceedings. "Welcome everyone, to this very precarious moment in the history of our city." He spoke with confidence and pride addressing an audience that overflowed into the halls. "I have chosen four individuals from hundreds of applicants, whom I feel have the most potential to be the rightful owner of this honorable puppy we are calling Pupster." The judge turned his attention to the four people standing in front of his podium. He continued, "I find it curious to note that Pupster has not responded affectionately with any of you. It is clear that there is one family with whom this puppy is attached." He broke his gaze with the claimants to give a brief look towards Sarah and her parents. "In either case, this must be solved legally." He looked at the claimants once more in the hope that they would give up their selfish reasons for wanting Pupster. Not one moved an inch or spoke a word towards giving up their claim of ownership, the Judge continued, "Very well then. Let us proceed."

Big Tex spoke first. "Well Mr. Judge. Seems to me that the dog belongs to me. I fed him and provided a good home for him at my shop. He showed up one day and kept coming back for at least a year. Tom, Pete, and Steve here can vouch for that!"

"Is this true?" asked the Judge. The three men nodded in agreement.

"Mom, what is happening? Is he really the owner?" asked Sarah. Her mom shook her head and shrugged her shoulders, but did not vocalize her answer as she was intent on listening to the proceedings.

The three other community members, one of which was from a town about 30 miles away, did not have a good case. They were clearly there to cash in on Pupster's notoriety. Judge Carter did not need much deliberation time. He made his decision quickly.

The crowd was silent as he spoke after hearing from each claimant. "It is my judgement that the person who fed the animal, provided shelter, and cared for him should be the permanent care taker. I decree that Big Tex take immediate ownership of the dog." With a pounding of the gavel, the decision was final.

As the crowd chattered amongst themselves, the bailiff brought out Pupster. Tears rolled down Sarah's cheeks as she watched her dear friend being handed to Big Tex.

Big Tex held up Pupster above his head. "There you are my little..." he paused to come up with a name. "...Gator. Yeah, I missed you a whole lot." Tex rambled on to a small crowd and reporters. He made up a story of how he saved Pupster from the clenches of an alligator. Nobody really cared to hear from him. They just wanted to know what he planned on doing with Pupster. He walked out of the court room carrying Pupster in his arms like a football. "No questions please." Tex, told the crowd.

Pupster looked back at Sarah who was turned around in her seat crying. "Sarah..." Pupster fought to free himself but he couldn't. Tex's grip was too strong. He gave up the fight and cried as he was carried out of the courtroom for an unknown future.

Dog Napped

Leaving the courthouse, Big Tex placed a collar around Pupster's neck and tethered him with a leash. For the first time in his life, Pupster felt like a prisoner. He trotted slowly next to Tex, occasionally looking back in search of Sarah.

They arrived at Tex's beat up old tow truck. Big Tex picked up Pupster placing him on the seat. He pulled out a dog biscuit from his pocket, throwing it at Pupster. It bounced off of Pupster's snout and landed on the floor mat. Pupster ignored the treat. As Pupster turned away from the snack, it started to rain. Tex carelessly knocked Pupster off the seat as he reached over to roll up the window. "Move out of the way you Mangy Mutt! I don't need you jumping out the window and running back to your girlfriend. Ha, ha, ha…"

Pupster was a very sad indeed!

Big Tex's cell phone rang. He scrambled back to his side fumbling with his phone as he rolled up the window on his side of the truck. He answered, "Hello. Who is this? Oh, hi. Yep. I got him. How much did you say? You think I'm stupid don't you? No, you shut up. Triple the original price and I might think about it." He clapped the phone shut and laughed greedily. "Stupid people ha, ha, ha... Let's go mutt. Time to see your new home!"

Back at the shop, Pupster was introduced to his new home. He was shoved into a dog kennel. "You ain't goin' nowhere now Mutt, or Gator, or Pupster... whatever your name is!" He knelt down and gave Pupster an exaggerated whining baby look. "You belong to me and I intend on making some good money from you." Big Tex sat back in his chair, kicked his feet up on the cooler, he used as a coffee table, and turned on the television. Killer was tied up outside. He peered through the glass door giving Pupster a death stare. Tex dozed off to the sound of

Monica Snyder's voice as she reported on the big stories of the day.

Deep in the night, Pupster was stirred from his sleep. He heard shuffling coming from the garage. A faint voice whispered in the night. "There he is." Pupster's eyes winced from a quick flash of light in his eyes. "Just grab the cage." Whispered a second voice.

Big Tex was sound asleep. Unfortunately for him, his snoring masked the sound of the trashcan being knocked over as the two robbers withdrew from the room. Killer silently watched as Pupster was carried away.

"Quick, put him in the trunk." Whispered one of the thieves. The truck door slammed shut, rattling the cage. With the cargo secure, the car drove off into the night.

Double Caught

One of the robbers looked strangely familiar. After a few minutes of bouncing back and forth in the trunk, Pupster remembered the guy. He was one of the persons who was trying to claim him during the court case. He strained to hear the muffled voices coming from the front but it wasn't of any use.

The driver looked in the rearview mirror and noticed a police car quickly approaching. He started to panic. "Oh darn. It's the cops. Stay cool man...stay cool."

The passenger screamed. "The red and blue lights are flashing! Pull over! No, don't pull over!" His friend realized they were not going to out run the cops. "Wait...pull over! Stop! Pull over, now!" They pulled over. The two men sat nervously anticipating the arrival of the officer to their window.

The police officer cautiously approached the

driver's side door. "License and registration, please." The officer calmly asked as she spoke to the men in the car. "Do you know why I pulled you over?"

The driver's hands were shaking uncontrollably as he passed the officer his documents. He could barely get the words out of his mouth, "No, Ma'am." His voice shook. "Was I driving too fast?"

The officer's reply was firm. "First, you were driving with your headlights off. I assumed you had car troubles. Then I noticed that your registration is expired. Finally, when I looked you up in the system I found that this car is registered to a Betty Sue Hollister. Are either one of you named Betty?" She began to get frazzled at the lack of respect these two were giving her. "You know what, I need you both to get out. Move to the front of the car and place your hands on the hood. Don't make me ask twice."

Pupster realized that the car had stopped. He was scared. He wanted nothing more but to be with his best friend. Pushing aside his fears he drew the strength to give a quick bark.

The police officer's reaction was immediate. She approached the driver, night stick in hand. "What do you have in the trunk? Is there a dog in the trunk? Open it, now!" The driver opened the trunk. The officer's light shined in Pupster's face.

"Officer, I can explain." The driver tried to speak. He then broke down crying inconsolably. "It was all my fault. This is my Grandma's car. I live with her. She doesn't know I have it. Please don't tell her. I beg you…" He went on and on as the police officer tried to make sense of the situation.

"Stop! Just stop crying." She said as she radioed in for support. "Dispatch, Squad 39. I have a routine stop that turned into a barrel of tangled monkeys. Going to need back up and animal control."

Dispatch replied. "Animal control? Sounds like a good call. Additional units will be on scene in less than 15 minutes."

Pupster knew exactly who the animal control was. "Oh man," he thought, "this has gone from bad to worse. These guys were always trying to grab me. Guess this is it! Well, maybe not, if I can play nice with the officer, perhaps I can get out of this cage."

Pupster began wagging his tail and jumping back and forth in the cage acting as if he wanted to play. The officer went over to the cage to find out what was going on in the trunk. "Are you okay, boy?" She asked. "Wait a minute! Aren't you the miracle dog? You look just like the one I saw on the news. Nah, you can't be him. He was turned over to his owner in the town down the road. If I open the cage are you going to bite me?"

"Bite you? Why would I bite you? I might kiss you and lick your face!" Pupster thought, barking in approval.

The officer reached down into the trunk to open

the cage door. As soon as the tension was off the latch, Pupster leaped for his freedom. The officer fruitlessly grabbed for him, but she could not hold to him. He was free! As soon as his paws touched the ground, he gained traction and sprinted away as fast as he could.

Into the darkness, under a fence, and through a field he ran. He ran and ran. He ran so far that the sound of the road was almost inaudible. He found himself alone again, free to go where he pleased. He looked up to take note of the twinkling things in the sky. It reminded him of his first home at the edge of town. His heart beat slowed, giving way to the sounds of crickets and frogs. He figured he was safe enough to be able to stop and rest.

The Long Road Home

"Cock-a-doodle-do…" Pupster woke up to the distant sound of a rooster's call. He looked around finding himself deep in a meadow. He stood up to get his bearings. The grass was too tall for him to see over. He tried jumping. Up and down he went attempting to get over the tufts of grass. He couldn't jump high enough. The only option he had was to walk in a straight line and hopefully find a clearing.

He walked for what seemed like hours eventually his surroundings began to change. He walked under a wooden fence emerging from out of the bush and into a clearing. Cautiously, he looked around. The last thing he wanted was to get caught again. He peeked his head into the clearing determining that it was safe, so he continued his journey. He approached a group of cows grazing in the field. "Hello, tall cow." He barked to the cow chewing her cud.

The cow looked down at him, continuing her chewing.

"Can you please tell me where I am? In which direction is the city? Oh, and do you know where I can get some water or some food?"

Again, the cow's only response was to chew. She shook her head a couple of times then twisted to the right. Since Pupster really didn't have any direction, he decided that this was her way of telling him to travel in that direction.

Appreciative and anxious to continue his journey back to Sarah, Pupster thanked the cow and walked along the fence line. It wasn't long before he found himself at the bank of a river.

The river was as wide as a football field. The water was fast moving and cold. He had no idea how he was going to get to the other side. He knew that crossing the river would be dangerous. It was way too deep to walk across and too wide to swim. He kneeled down next to the bank to take a drink.

After his drink, he paced back and forth trying to figure out his next move. He could go back the way he came, eat some grass with the cows, then probably get lost again. If by chance he found his way back to the road, he still didn't know which way to go. The most direct path back to town seemed to be crossing the river.

He rested under the drooping branches of a willow tree pondering his circumstances and thinking of Sarah. He started to doze off when he noticed some creatures hopping on the water's edge. Curiosity got the best of him.

Crawling on his belly, he slowly moved to the water's edge. He was able to get close to some frogs who were hopping around and conversing. They sat for a while in the shallow water with their eyeballs sticking out of the water. "Croak, ribbit, ribbit," went one frog, then a minute later, another would repeat.

Occasionally, they would hop to different spots. It was interesting but not enough to keep his attention. Then he noticed the sticks and logs floating down the river. In the distance, he heard the echoing of the frogs, "Croak, ribbit, ribbit." Then, like a flash of lightning, a thought came to him. He could be a frog. He might be able to jump from log to branch to get to the other side.

"Thank you, frogs!" he barked. He startled the frogs causing them to jump into deeper water and hide.

Executing the plan was going to be more difficult than hatching it. He scanned up river to see what branches were coming his way. He saw what he thought was a good bunch. He mentally prepared himself, crouching in a ready position to leap for the first target.

"Okay. I can do this! I am a dog...I am a dog...I am a frog. What? What am I saying? Yeah...I'm a frog. Think like a frog." He told himself over and over. "Okay, you are the super hero dog that saved Sarah. The whole town believes in you. Now, believe in yourself. On the count of three...one, two, three!"

Pupster jumped, stretching his legs as far as they could go. He landed safely on a wood plank. It was wobbly but firm. The only problem now was that there was nowhere else to go. He was left floating down the river. He looked back and saw the willow tree getting smaller as the river carried him away.

If things weren't bad enough the sky grew dark, the clouds gathered and it began to rain. The river was getting rougher by the minute. Pupster's tiny little life raft began to twist and teeter from the rough water. He frantically scanned the river for branches, tree trunks, anything that would help him get closer to the other side. Nothing was within reach. He grew more and more desperate with every passing second.

'FLASH!' went the lightning. The wind was

pushing him to the edge of his board. Through the dense wall of rain he saw an opportunity. One tiny glimmer of hope. A log halfway between him and the shore was drifting his way. If he could leap to it, surely he would be close enough to the shore to be able to swim to safely to the other side.

The log was moving faster than he thought. He had to act fast. It was now within range. He didn't have time to count to three. He had to act now! He jumped for the log. His hind paws slipped taking away some of his thrust. He landed in the water barely grasping onto the edge of the log. Pupster pawed and scratched with his claws trying to get atop the log. It was no use. The log spun every time he pulled on it. Pupster held tight with his claws dug deep into the bark. His snout barely above water. He was shivering from the cold and afraid for his life. As he bobbed up and down through the rocky water his thoughts remained fixed. His one goal was to get back to his best friend Sarah. She is what gave him the strength to hold on. 'CRACK!' Went the thunder. A flash of light jolted him back to his situation. He looked around and saw a large rock splitting the stream. Would it be more detrimental to stay in the water attached to the spinning log or would it be best to try to get to the only dry spot in the middle of the river. He was desperate and freezing. He let go of the log in the hopes of catching the rock. The current dragged him under the water. He hit his head and bounced off the rock. The river proved to be too powerful.

Pupster paddled for the surface only to be knocked down by branches and other debris. He fought his way to the top, grabbed a breath of air only to be pulled down again. "Sarah…I have to get to Sarah!" Were his thoughts just before being knocked on the head by a heavy log. His motionless body drifted deep into the darkness, being dragged under by the powerful current.

Sarah's Search

"Wait up, baby girl." Sarah's mom huffed as she grabbed her purse, car keys and flyers in a mad dash out the door. Sarah had a bundle of flyers with Pupster's picture. The flyer read:

Missing Friend...

$100 Reward...

Call 555-2324 to report any sighting

She was well ahead of her mom handing out the flyers in the neighborhood. She stopped to post the flyer at nearly every tree.

"Slow down Sarah. We have all day. It has only

been twenty minutes and I am already getting tired." Monica had to figure out a way to get Sarah to pace herself. "Tell you what. Let's stop at the café. I will get coffee and you can have an orange juice. Then we will be able to put signs around the downtown area where most people will be."

Sarah paused while stapling a flyer. After briefly evaluating the option, she agreed. "Mmm…okay. We have to hurry though, because it's going to be lunch time soon. I want as many people as possible to see these posters."

At the café, the buzz in the room was again with the little miracle dog. Today's chatter involved the mysterious circumstances behind the dog napping. It was in the newspaper, on the local network news and being passed on through social media. In fact, Sarah's mom was doing a short story about it for the evening news.

Sarah sat at the table next to the window. She put

her head down on the table to gaze at the people and cars as they passed by. One vehicle caught her attention. It was Big Tex's truck. She immediately perched up with the hopes of catching a glimpse of Pupster. Big Tex was alone, his fishing poles stuck out the window of the passenger's side window.

Sarah's mom interrupted her gaze when she sat down with the drinks. Sarah told her mom exactly what was on her mind. "You know Mom. It isn't right that Big Tex is the owner of Pupster. He doesn't even care about him. He didn't even care enough to keep him safe. Look, there he goes." She pointed at the truck as it passed. "Looks like he is going fishing. He isn't even looking for him. He doesn't deserve Pupster!" Clearly upset, nearly in tears she continued, "I'm glad that Pupster is gone."

Monica tried to put her at ease. "I know you don't mean that. You have to admit, that it was a little comforting to know where Pupster was. Maybe he cares in a different way than you or I?"

"No!" Sarah snapped, hitting her hands on the table. She startled the other customers. She continued her rant with tears running down her cheeks. "I know for a fact. We are out here doing everything that we can do to find Pupster. He doesn't care. I just saw him driving by with fishing poles in his truck. He is going fishing when he should be out looking for Pupster!"

Sarah's mom went around to the other side of the table to sit next to her. Monica hugged her. She held her tight and told her that it was going to be okay. She reassured her that she and her daddy were going to do everything that they could do to find Pupster. Together they sat and shed a few tears.

An Unfortunate Rescue

"Oh my goodness. The river must have flooded." A jubilant Tex said to himself as he stood on the river bank overlooking the accumulation of washed up trash and broken branches. "I am eating catfish tonight! Woohoo!" He sang as he twirled into an impromptu dance.

He set up quickly as he didn't want to lose the opportunity for a good catch. He plopped down his folding chair. Placed his ice chest. Sprayed some bug spray on his jacket and bare legs. He baited two fishing poles, casted them out and then sat anticipating catching a great big fish.

Thirty minutes passed with no bites. Tex was getting inpatient and a little hungry. He got up to grab a bag of chips from his truck. He returned to find one of his poles had fallen. Excited, he ripped open the bag, shoving a fist full of chips into his mouth and then leaped for the pole. He yanked hard to set the hook. "It's a big one!" he shouted. Bits of potato chip crumbs flew from his mouth. This was going to be the biggest fish he had ever landed. He fought a good fight. He pulled hard, taking in the slack, resting and repeating until the trophy fish was close to shore.

"Well...I never!" exclaimed Tex. He had been fighting with a broken tree branch. Tangled in the branches was a seemingly lifeless dog. "Mutt, is that you?" He bent down to pick up and inspect the shivering wet dog. Pupster was exhausted. He looked up at Big Tex then closed his eyes letting his head fall. Tex took off his fishing vest to use it to warm up Pupster. He placed him on the floor of the passenger side of his truck. He packed up his things then drove off. Not quite a mile away from the river Big Tex pulled out his cell phone to call his cousin Robert. "Rob...I got him! It's the Mutt. You are not going to believe where I found him. Quiet! I need a favor. Do you still have internet service?"

"Sure do. Why?" Robert replied.

"Because, I have to get rid of this dog quickly. He's too hot. There are still a lot of people who want him. Going to sell him on the internet. I will be at your house in twenty minutes. Have some water and food ready for the mangy mutt. He looks bad. Thanks." He ended the conversation and placed the phone on the seat.

Pupster had no idea what was going on. He was thankful to be out of the water. He was too exhausted to run. He laid his head down and fell asleep.

Breaking News

Cuddled tightly on the couch with her daddy munching on some popcorn, Sarah was ready to watch her favorite news show, Channel 7 News. Her mom was doing a special segment to ask the community to keep a look out for their lost friend.

George, the co-anchor, opened the segment with a haughty tone. "Good evening, Monica. How about that weather? The recent rainy days have been atrocious."

"Indeed, it was a nasty storm that brought the water levels of the river to new heights, George. Is there any damage to report?" Monica responded.

"Thankfully not. The spillways were able to manage the flooding this time. On a positive note, I did hear that if you are a fisherman, the rise in waters may be in your favor." As he continued his general banter, a note was passed to Monica.

Monica's face lit up with concern. She interrupted George with breaking news. "I am sorry to interrupt you, George, but this just came in. The miracle dog has been found." She paused to calm her excitement. "Apparently, he was recovered from the river." Her excitement turned to horror as she read the final portion of the note. "His owner has placed an ad online to sell Pupster. This should be good news to anyone who is interested in owning our home town hero." Monica's elation quickly turned to sadness knowing that her family was at home watching. In an effort to calm her child's emotions, whom she knew was watching, she closed the breaking news report with these words…"At least we know he is safe."

Sarah jumped from her dad's side knocking the popcorn from his hands. She screamed, "PUPSTER!" She was happy to hear Pupster was safe, but devastated that he was back with mean old Big Tex. She couldn't hold in her emotions. She ran to her room, jumped into her bed and covered her head with her covers.

While Sarah was working out her emotions, her mom was doing what she could to get Pupster back. She stopped by Big Tex's shop on her way home from work. After knocking on the front door of the shop she called out, "Big Tex are you in?"

Tex came to the door, hesitantly opening it for Monica. "What do you want? Are you looking for a news story?"

Monica was taken back by his frankness and harsh tone. "I'm afraid not." She took a brief moment to gather her thoughts. "We have known each other since grade school. I have never asked you for anything. But I need your help now."

Tex staired at her without any emotion showing in his face. He held on to the door, poised to close it at any moment.

Monica continued, "That little dog you have in your care has a very special bond with my daughter. I would like to take him home. What will it take?" Sarah asked almost pleading.

Tex loosened his stance, removing his hand from the door. He allowed it to open a little wider. "Monica. I just got off the phone with my cousin. He is keeping track of the bids for the dog. It is outrageous." The more he spoke on the subject, the more excitement he started to show. "I thought I could get a couple of hundred dollars for him, but the highest bid right now is TEN THOUSOUND DOLLARS! If you want this dog you are going to have to match the highest bidder."

Monica looked at him, knowing that she could not pay that amount. She felt as if he was asking for a ransom for a kidnapped family member. She grudgingly thanked him for his time. She didn't let her true feelings show. As she turned away the tears began to fall. At her car door, she wiped her tears then got into the vehicle.

Big Tex waited for her to get into her car before he shut his door. He kept a look out from the window to make sure she left his property. He went back to his chair where Killer rested next to him on the floor. He slowly scratched behind the German Shepherd's ears as they both stared at Pupster, who was safely in a cage sitting on top of the television.

The Deal is Done

"Hi, I'm Monica Snyder, and we are live at the local café, where local repairman, affectionately known as Big Tex, is patiently waiting for the buyer of his dog, whom I like to call, Pupster. He has been sold for the outstanding price of ten thousand dollars." Standing next to her was Tex, dressed in a new suit topped off with a fancy cowboy hat. "Tell me, Big Tex, how does it feel to sell this little puppy to the highest bidder? How have you lived with yourself for the last few days waiting for the auction to end?" It was clear that she was agitated and acting slightly passive-aggressive with her guest. "I mean, how does it feel to be so fortunate that someone is willing to pay so much for such a small dog?"

Tex was oblivious to Monica's rude comments. He kept watching the door waiting for the buyer. "Well Monica, to be honest, I wasn't expecting such a spectacle. Look at the little mutt." He pointed towards

Pupster who was tied up to the bar stool. Pupster sat quietly, unaware of his future. "He is a scrawny little thing. Why someone would pay so much for him, I do not know!"

"Why are we here Tex?" shouted a person from the crowd.

"I called you all because I felt this was news worthy. You know, the dog being a special dog and all." Tex was visibly uncomfortable with being the center of attention. He continued fumbling over his own words. "He...uh...kinda belongs to us all, you know? In a way. So, I wanted to share the sale of OUR dog with you all. I don't know. I thought it was, well, a community thing. It just felt right. You know?"

Monica jumped on his comment. "So what you are telling me, is that the dog belongs to the community and not to you?"

Tex was uncomfortable, but not unwise, he could

not be driven into a battle of wits. "Oh…Monica, you know that's not what I meant. The judge said he is mine, so I have the right to sell him. You journalists! Always trying to make something out of nothing." He laughed as he looked towards the door.

Looking directly into the camera, Monica continued her dialogue. "Any minute now the proud new owner of our little hero dog is going to walk through the door. Who will it be? Will it be the mayor? The Chief of Police? Or will it be some mysterious representative of a wealthy benefactor who does not want to be identified? The tension is almost unbearable." Truly, it was unbearable for her. For she knew that in a few moments her little girl was going to lose her best friend, perhaps, forever.

The doorbell chimed, signaling the entrance of a new customer. The door opened. Everyone stood quiet to see who had walked in. It was Sarah!

Bought & Paid For

Sarah was shocked by the amount of people stuffed in the café. She walked in slowly, realizing that everyone was staring at her. Pupster got excited catching a glimpse of Sarah. He tugged at the leash trying to free himself.

Monica immediately gave her attention to her daughter. "Um, ladies and gentlemen I have to take a brief break." She gestured to the cameraman to keep rolling because they were live. "Thank you all for your patience." Monica quickly turned off her professional role to put on her mommy hat. She pulled her to the side. "Why aren't you at home? Where's your daddy?

At their home, Sarah's dad spit out his coffee at the sight of Sarah on the news. He screamed, "That girl is going to be the death of me!" He threw his coffee cup in the sink and grabbed his car keys, immediately making his way to the café.

In her mom's presence, Sarah began crying hysterically. "I lied. I am so sorry. I just couldn't lose him."

Monica was confused, but let Sarah continue pouring out her feelings.

"He is my best friend. I logged in and used your credit card to make a profile so that I could bid on Pupster."

Monica's heart skipped a beat at the news of Sarah's indiscretion but she remained calm. Her only focus was to support her broken-hearted child.

Sarah continued, "I love him, Mommy. I can't live without him. I didn't know this was going to be such a big deal. I was going to give Mr. Tex my piggy bank and promise him all my allowance from now until I am thirty. I can't live without him. I can't! I can't lose him again!!!"

Monica held her tight to calm her down. "Sarah, catch your breath baby. I need you to trust me. No matter what happens, I need you to know that Pupster is going to be okay."

Sarah was a bit confused. She looked over at Pupster then back to her mom. She was puzzled.

Monica held out her hand. "Please hand me your piggy bank."

Sarah passed it over wiping her tears. As she did, her dad walked through the door. He pushed through the crowd to get to his little girl.

Monica returned her attention to the live report and to the crowd. "Well folks. This is the big climax that you've all been waiting for. Apparently," she paused, "it was my daughter who made the offer to purchase Pupster for ten thousand dollars." She looked straight into the camera, held up the piggy bank, then took a few steps towards Tex. "Before you pass judgement, please consider that my daughter named this dog." She gestured towards Pupster. The camera focused on Pupster who was fighting to free himself from the leash. Sarah went to his side to calm him down. The camera returned to Monica. "This dog saved her life. In turn, she nursed him back to life after he was mortally injured."

Big Tex squirmed. The look on his face was quickly turning to shame.

Monica continued, "She is the only one in this dog's life who has never asked anything of him. She is not trying to profit from him. All she wants is to give him love." She turned to Tex to speak to him directly. "Tex, she loves him. Can't you see?"

Tex lowered his eyes to the ground.

Monica continued her passionate plea. "Big Tex, on behalf of my daughter I apologize for this mistake. We can't pay you ten thousand dollars. But I will offer you two hundred dollars plus whatever is saved up in this piggy bank. Do we have a deal?"

Tex's momentary look of shame quickly turned to anger. Big Tex threw his hands up in the air and shouted, "NO DEAL!"

The crowd was stunned.

Monica pulled the piggy bank close to her body in preparation for an angry rant.

Tex allowed the silence to linger before opening his mouth to address the crowd. "In all my years, I have not been given such a great opportunity like this one. Two hundred dollars will not pay my bills. I have a business to keep up and a vacation to plan. This isn't about you, your little girl, or this community. This is about ME!"

On those words the crowd began to heckle and forcefully express their dislike for Tex's response to the situation.

With another shout, Tex tried to hush the crowd a second time, but they didn't respond like the first time. The crowd's dissatisfaction with Tex only grew stronger.

In the midst of the arguing and dissatisfaction was a little girl and a homeless dog. Sarah knelt down on her knees to embrace Pupster. She held him tight not knowing if this would be their last day together.

Then a change came over the crowd. It was started by one man who raised his hands to get everyone's attention. "Listen up…everyone, listen to me!" The crowd settled down enough for the individual to be heard. "I have twenty dollars here, I am donating this to Tex for the sake of Sarah and Pupster." He waved the bill in the air and continued talking. "These two belong together. Will you join me? Will you help me to unite these two once and for all?" He walked up to Tex, looked him straight in the eyes, then dropped the money at his feet. He then turned and walked out of the café.

Tex stared at the money on the ground. He had no intentions of picking it up. He remained still, stern and quiet.

Monica was at a loss for words while the cameraman captured the intensity of the moment.

The crowd remained quiet while they processed what had just happened. Then, one by one people began digging in their pockets, purses and wallets. Individually, each person dropped their donation at Tex's feet then left the café. Eventually, he was left standing in the center of a mound of money.

Tex continued staring at his feet processing what was happening. He didn't fully understand why these strangers were dropping their money in support of reuniting Sarah and Pupster. Then, in a single yet simple act, his resolve began to break. He dropped his shoulders. Then came the final blow.

Monica and her husband slowly approached the big man. Monica kneeled down and placed the piggy bank atop the mound of money then stood up and took a couple steps back. Her husband embraced her.

They patiently waited for Tex's reaction. That's when it happened.

A single tear drop fell from the hardened eyes of the big man standing in the middle of a pile of money. Then came the second tear, then a third. Tex fell to his knees and cried.

Moved with compassion, Sarah walked over to him and placed her arm on his shoulder. "Mr. Tex," she spoke from her heart, "it's going to be alright!"

Tex reached up and hugged her. He held her tight. Then he did the unthinkable. He asked Sarah to forgive him for his greedy stubbornness. "Sarah, honey, I'm sorry for the way I behaved. Please forgive me. I didn't mean any harm to you or to the mutt, I mean…Pupster. I was just being greedy. You have fought tooth and nail for this dog. All the time I was blind. I failed to realize how much love you have for each other." He raised his head to look her straight in her eyes. "I want you to have him!"

Sarah shouted in joy. She gave Tex a great big hug. Then she turned and hugged her parents. Finally, she ran to Pupster, gave him a kiss and untied him. From that very moment Pupster remained at her side. Sarah and Pupster left the store to walk home while her mom finished the news cast.

The Stroll Home

Sarah wiped the tears from her eyes as she and Pupster walked out of the cafe. Pupster matched her stride looking up at her as they walked home. Sarah decided to take the short cut through the woods.

Sarah chatted with Pupster as they walked. "I can't believe this is finally over. You get to come home and stay with me forever. I couldn't bear to live without you, Pupster. You are my best friend."

Pupster barked back as if he was actively involved in the conversation. "It sure is great to be back with you, Sarah. I wish you could understand me. I can't believe I'm here with you right now. Sarah, I've never had a family. You're my family. Guess what else? I love you!"

Sarah responded, "I love you too!"

Pupster stopped on the trail and looked at Sarah

with a puzzled look. "Did you just answer me?"

Sarah kept walking. "Come on boy. We'll be home soon." Just then the clouds began to gather. The wind kicked up and it started to rain. Sarah and Pupster ran to a treehouse just off the trail. She grabbed her little friend with one arm and climbed into the fort. Then it started to hail. The strength of the wind caused the massive trees to sway back and forth. Sarah peeked out of the window to see a circular cloud forming in the sky. She grabbed Pupster and crouched into the corner.

At the cafe, the news of a tornado touching down on the edge of town broke up the party. Everyone clambered for safety running behind the bar and diving under tables. Monica made a dash for the door trying to run after her daughter. Big Tex and her husband grabbed her pulling her back into the restaurant. Just then a newspaper stand flew past the door.

Monica leaped for the door again, only to be restrained once more. She screamed for her daughter, "SARAH!"

To Be Continued...

Ari's Struggle

Ari is short for Ariadne. She was born on the Air Force Base in Misawa, Japan. She came into the world as the most peaceful child. She was the perfect baby. She didn't fuss much unless she was hungry or messy. One of her favorite things to do was to sit in her bouncy chair. She was such a delight.

As delightful as she was, and still is, we didn't know that school was going to be such a great challenge for her. She had a very difficult time with reading, math and staying organized. Homework was always a chore, taking up most of the evening for her to complete.

My wife and I thought that the problem was that she was not focused and unmotivated. We did everything that we could do to try to keep her on track. We would clean her room with her. We established a written schedule for her, while pleading with her to keep track of her own tasks. The only way that she would finish anything was with direct supervision.

So, in my infinite wisdom, I came up with this idea that my child wasn't lazy, but merely disinterested in the characters and stories that she was encountering in the books that she was reading. In an attempt to help improve her reading skills, I decided to collaborate with her on a writing project. Her task was to help me develop characters for a story that we would write together. That is how Pupster was born.

The process was slow. It was difficult finding time in between homework and keeping her room clean, but we made it work. About halfway through the development of the story we were given some very difficult news.

The news we received came from Ari's third grade teacher. He brazenly told us that she was probably experiencing Attention Deficit Disorder. We were shocked, in disbelief and questioned the teacher's motivation. He stated that he had ADD as a child, that he still was affected by it and that we needed to immediately get our child on medication. His advice was not well received.

Partially due to personal denial but mostly due to the teachers brash approach, we didn't accept his advice. We felt that Ari was just a "late bloomer." Both her mom and I struggled in school. We figured that it was normal for her to struggle a bit. We fully expected her to eventually catch up with her peers. Inevitably, we did not get her looked at for the possibility of being diagnosed with ADD until later.

We literally fought our way through grade school. In hind sight, she probably should have been held back a year. If she was in a public school, she probably would've been held back at least one of those years. Junior high was when we finally embraced the truth.

Midway into her eighth grade year, the guidance counselor approached us with a serious concern. She had been observing Ari as she struggled through the beginning of the year. She compassionately approached us asking us to consider having Ari screened for ADD. At this point, we were at our wits end. All we wanted was for our precious baby girl to have a chance to succeed. We knew she had the will and mental capacity but she didn't seem to have the ability to focus.

We had her diagnosed. The results confirmed that she had ADD. This is where everything changed for her. Almost immediately, with treatment, she exhibited a 180 degree turn. She learned the skills that she needed to stay on task and was able to catch up and even surpass her peers in some subjects. She is bright, intelligent and strong.

Pupster is an analogy of our daughter's will power to overcome life's adversities. We hope that you enjoy this unique story that was born out of love for a struggling daughter. Love conquers all. May Pupster captivate your heart as he has captivated ours.

Final Thoughts...

I hope that you loved every moment of this heart-felt story. If you absolutely adore this book, will you do me the honor of telling others about it? Please tell the whole world! I don't have the power of a publishing company backing me. Anything that you do to help share Pupster is extremely appreciated.

A few ways to reach me:

- Visit my *Amazon Author Page* (Tavio Soto)

- *Email* – thepupsterbook@gmail.com

- *Instagram* @thepupsterbook

- *TikTok* @Pupsterbook

Stay tuned, Pupster's adventures will continue!

Made in the USA
Middletown, DE
30 October 2022

13778147R00076